THE MARAKON WAYS

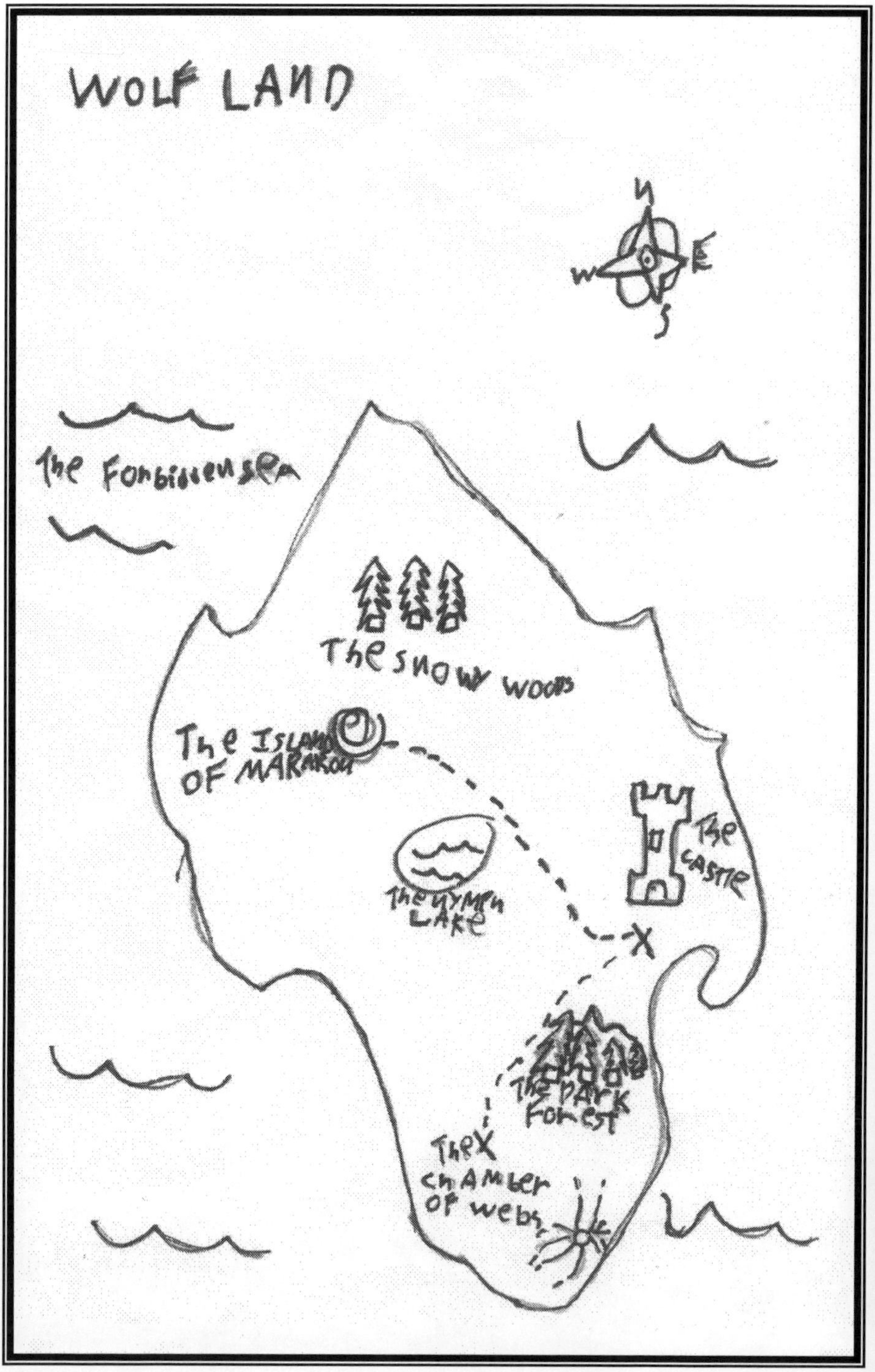
WOLF LAND
N
W
E
S
The Fonbiddensea
The snow woods
The ISLAND OF MARAKOU
The nymph LAKE
The castle
X
The Dark Forest
The X chamber of webs

BOOK I

THE MARAKON WAYS

Written by Griffin Hehmeyer
Illustrated by Matt's Class

Teemeyer Press
Bellevue, WA

A portion of the proceeds from the sale of this book is donated to The Little School in Bellevue, Washington.

Published in the United States by:

◠ Teemeyer Press
13109 NE 38th Place
Bellevue, WA 98005
http://www.teemeyer.org

First Edition
ISBN 978-0-9893572-0-3

To everybody who has been my friend
and my family in my entire life.

TABLE OF CONTENTS

PROLOGUE

Throughout the different dimensions, there are portals that lead from one dimension to another. Most of these are very well hidden. This story is about how one was discovered. At that time, there was a war going on. This is also a story about the adventures of Lily and Daniel. They learn many things and make new discoveries for the world.

Chapter 1

THE VORTEX KANGAROO

"Daniel, stop it!" said Lily. Daniel was pretending to be a lion and eat Lily's lunch. (They were at the zoo.)

Their mom, Shelly, said, "Daniel, stop annoying your sister. We're going to see the kangaroo now." Daniel and Lily groaned. The kangaroo was always, ALWAYS the most boring part of the zoo.

As they got closer to the kangaroo, Daniel started to pretend to be a boa constrictor and pretended he was going to crush Lily's guts out. Lily said, "Stop!" and this time Daniel obeyed.

This freaked Lily out, because for eleven years her older brother Daniel had always seemed to annoy her. Although she had said, "Stop!" many times, Daniel had never once actually stopped. When Lily looked up, she saw why he did this time. Daniel was frozen in his tracks, staring at a wolf, A WOLF, in the kangaroo pen. Even weirder, the kangaroo and the wolf were together in the pen and the kangaroo was not being eaten. Weirdest of all, the wolf vanished into thin air. And right before he vanished, he looked like a young man, a very tall one, with dark brown hair, and light grey skin.

When they got home, Lily and Daniel told their mom about what they had seen at the zoo. Their mom just said, "Oh, what an active imagination you kids have."

That night, right before bed, Lily heard a howl (HOWWWLLL) outside of her bedroom window. But when she looked outside, she saw nothing except the pitch-black sky. In the morning Daniel reported that he had heard a howl, too. Their mom said, "It must have been the neighbor's dog, because there are no wolves for miles around here, unless you count the zoo."

The next day at school Lily and Daniel both got in trouble for presenting oral reports about the things they had seen at the zoo. Their teachers said it must have been a dream, and gave them each an F-minus. When their mom heard about this she was furious. She said, "We're not going to the zoo EVER EVER EVER again!" But because of the strange events at the kangaroo pen, Lily and Daniel really wanted to return to the zoo that same day. So they begged their mom to please let them.

Eventually their mom relented and said that they could go to the zoo if they wanted to, but she refused to go with them. This could have been a problem, but Daniel was sixteen and had just received his driver's license six weeks ago. Lily and Daniel got in the car. As they drove, Daniel imagined that they were on their way to have an adventure, because he thought the wolf-man would be there again and was probably from an unknown land. Lily imagined that they would have a normal afternoon at the zoo and that nothing unusual would happen. But darn was she wrong!

When they got to the zoo, Lily and Daniel immediately went to see the kangaroo. At first they only saw the kangaroo in the kangaroo pen. But then they saw a wolf in the pen, too. And, just like before, they saw the wolf transform into a human, the same one they had seen before. As they remembered, the wolf-man had light grey skin, dark brown hair, and was very tall.

Lily and Daniel were curious to learn more about what was going on in the kangaroo pen. Lily made a plan to sneak into the pen and learn more. She whispered it into Daniel's ear. Following her plan, Lily and Daniel took their positions. Daniel climbed to the roof of the pen and tried to pry open the top. Meanwhile Lily distracted the wolf and the kangaroo with eye vine grapes, the kangaroo's favorite food. Eventually Daniel managed to break open the cage. Plop! Daniel fell right in.

Right when he did, the wolf and the kangaroo disappeared.

Confused, Daniel climbed out of the pen and rejoined Lily. The two of them looked around to see if there was someone who had seen the same things they had, but there was no one else there. Then they noticed something else. It was midnight! They had been at the zoo for eight hours.

"Our mom is going to be very angry at us," Daniel said to Lily. "Let's get home right away."

When they got home, they saw that their mom was not angry, but she was worried. "Where were you?" she asked. When Lily and Daniel told her they had been at the zoo the whole time, she said, "I called the zoo when you didn't come home, and learned that the zoo was closed today." She added sarcastically, "There must have been some secret magic at the zoo for you to break in without even noticing it. The zoo also told me that the kangaroo alarm got set off this afternoon, and I'm pretty sure I know who did it. YOU'RE GROUNDED!"

"Noooooooooooooooooooooooooooooooooooo!" said Lily.

"Nooooooooooooooooooo!" said Daniel just as Lily had said.

"Yes," said Mom. "Go to your room."

Lily and Daniel hung their heads and walked up the stairs. When they reached the landing, Daniel asked, "Why are we grounded?"

"I don't know," said Lily. "I don't even understand what happened. How did we get into the zoo if it was locked? And how did we stay for eight hours without even noticing?"

Then they heard a voice in Daniel's room. Daniel peeked in, and saw the tall grey man, the same one they saw at the zoo. But before they could even say a word, he vanished for a third time. Lily and Daniel stared at each other. Then a grin went across Lily's and Daniel's faces. They had a plan!

Chapter 2

SPYING AT THE ZOO

After their mom went to bed, Lily and Daniel stayed awake for many hours, discussing their plan to learn about the wolf-man and making it better. Finally, Daniel said they should get going. They had decided to disobey their mom, who had grounded them, and sneak out the window to the zoo using the old beat up collapsible ladder that Aunt Moonda had given Daniel for his thirteenth birthday. Daniel put the ladder through the window. As he started to climb, Lily noticed it was broken. She tried to warn her brother, but it was too late. Snap! Daniel hung by two fingers at the edge of the window as the ladder plummeted down to the ground.

"Hang on!" yelled Lily.

She ran downstairs as fast as she could to her parents' bedroom and yelled to her mom, panting and out of breath, "Daniel's going to fall." Lily was so scared that she could not say a word more, even if her life depended on it. Lily and Shelly ran upstairs. When Shelly saw Daniel she gasped at the sight and instantly helped him climb up. When Daniel was safe inside she said, "Now you're GROUNDED FOR LIFE!"

"Noooooooooooooooooooooooooooooooooooooooooooooooooo ooooooooooooooooooooooooooooooooooooooooooooooooooooooo ooooooooooooooooooooooooooooooooooooooooooooooooooooooo oooooo!" yelled Lily and Daniel.

"Yes," said Mom. Then their mom disappeared.

"What?" said Daniel.

"Yesssssss," said a loud hissing voice.

"Aaaaah!" screamed Daniel. When Daniel and Lily looked again, they saw a ghostly figure where their mom had been. This figure was different from the wolf-man. He had big black horns, dark black skin that shimmered in the wind, and two giant black wings on his back.

The ghostly figure hissed in his deep booming voice, "If you ever want to see your mom alive, come to the kangaroo pen at the zoo. Bye, for now."

Daniel and Lily rolled their eyes. They were certain they must be dreaming. At some point they would wake up and find everyone, Mom included, quietly back in their house. So they pinched each other to wake themselves up. "Owww!" said Lily and Daniel. They obviously weren't dreaming. This was real.

Lily and Daniel ran to the car, but to their surprise it didn't work, even though they had driven it to the zoo that same day. "Nooo!" cried Daniel. So Lily and Daniel got on their bikes and rode to the zoo instead. It took them a lot longer than driving would have, but at least they got to the zoo as quickly as possible. It was now very early in the morning, and the sun was just starting to rise.

Daniel and Lily got off their bikes and hooked them up to the bike rack. Daniel noticed that there was no one else at the zoo. Lily reminded Daniel that the zoo had not yet opened. But then Daniel remembered another thing. Since the zoo was closed, there would be guards at the zoo. They would have to sneak in or, and Lily and Daniel called it, "spy in."

Spying usually refers to the process of collecting information without being seen, but Daniel and Lily considered what they were about to do a kind of spying. "Well, why?" you ask. Well, because they were doing it to learn information. Learning about what had happened to their mom and about the disappearing man. And, even more importantly, they were doing it like an adventure. Now when I say "like an adventure," I mean unexpected things were about to happen. So while you might say what they were doing was sneaking in, I say it was more like spying. So Daniel and Lily spied (or, as you would say, sneaked) past the guards at the entrance to the zoo.

After they got past the guards, they came face to face with a giant fence. Daniel thought he could climb it, but Lily was a little bit worried because Daniel had already almost died once today. After Daniel fell down off the fence for the seventh time, Lily suggested they should try another way. She pointed to a little opening through the middle of the fence.

Daniel said, "Ha! I saw that before you. I just wanted to play with you and have some fun climbing the fence."

"Whatever!" said Lily.

They both squeezed through the hole as quickly as they could. PLOP! PLOP! They fell right through to the other side. But with the noise the two guards noticed them.

"Ruuunnnn!" Lily yelled to Daniel.

As they ran, the guards ran, too. Lily and Daniel ran faster than they ever had before. Eventually they came face to face with a wall.

"We've got you now!" said the guards. "You are going to be in big trouble when we talk to your parents!"

Then the guards disappeared.

"What?" asked Lily. "Why does that keep happening?"

"Well, at least it was a good thing this time," said Daniel. "We had better go to the kangaroo pen and rescue our mom."

So Lily and Daniel ran to the kangaroo pen. When they got there, they saw the big black horned ghostly figure again with their mom.. and the guards?!

"What?" said Lily, "Three people are in the pen today? And none of them are the wolf-man."

"Why did you want us to come here?" Daniel asked the ghostly figure.

The ghostly figure snarled in ghastly voice, and said, "If you ever want to see your mom, you must answer this riddle. When the three helms push, does the person bleed red blood or blue blood?"

Daniel and Lily didn't understand this question at all, so they made a guess.

"Purple blood," said Daniel.

"How did you know that the three helms made the person bleed purple blood?" said the ghostly figure in a ghastly voice. As he spoke, a portal opened and their mom teleported away with the guards. Lily and Daniel had a happy feeling that their mom and the guards had been transported back to their house.

Then the ghostly figure prepared to leave. "Your mom may be home, but you will never see her again," the ghostly figure said.

Because right then, he sucked them into another portal and they landed in a snowy woods.

Chapter 3

THE LAND

"Uhhhh..," said Lily and Daniel.

"Where are we?" asked Daniel.

"I don't know," replied Lily.

Lily and Daniel were in a big forest. The trees had no leaves and they were surrounded by snow. There were so many hills it was impossible for them to see very far. But between two hills they could see a big, frozen lake in the distance.

The two of them walked to the lake. When they got there, they saw a wolf-like creature. It looked like a wolf, but it walked on its hind legs and its front paws were hands. It was also shorter than a normal wolf. It howled at them and started to eye them like they were its prey.

Another creature, this time very mouse-like, came by. The wolf-like creature pounced on the mouse-like creature, and started to rip out the mouse-like creature's insides.

This gave Lily and Daniel enough time to escape around the lake. As they ran, they began to be able to see a little bit of a castle in the distance. As they drew closer, they were able to see the castle more clearly. Continuing on, they were eventually able to see an entire village. There was a big castle in the back, and many, many little huts before it.

Lily and Daniel thought they would be safe in the village. But then they heard, "Aaawwwwooooooo, aaawwwwoooooooooooo..," the sounds of wolves. Out of all of the huts came wolves. Out of one hut came the same gray man with the same dark hair that they saw two days earlier at the kangaroo pen. This time, the tall gray man talked to them.

He said in a soft voice, "Well, hello. I see that you have found a vortex to this place, which is called Wolf Land. There aren't just wolves here anymore, because now you are also here."

Lily and Daniel were stunned by everything they had just seen. They were even more stunned when all the wolves transformed into humans. The gray man looked stunned, too. It was like everybody was frozen. Not because anyone (besides Lily and Daniel) was surprised, but because of an old-looking man who came out of the castle. The old man yelled, "Arclon, what are you doing talking to a stranger?"

"Sorry, Dad. I just wanted to chat with humans," replied Arclon, the gray man.

"Come in and practice the Marakon Ways. NOW!! You haven't done it in a week!" said the old man.

"Uhhhh..," said Lily and Daniel. They didn't know what was going on.

"And, I give my apologies to you," said the old man. "because it seems like you are confused. You may be wondering what the Marakon Ways are. Come in and I will show you." Lily and Daniel didn't know what to do. So they went with the old man into the castle. When they got in, they were amazed at the size of the castle. They were in a large room with thousands of rooms on each side. There were twenty chandeliers that were hanging from the ceiling.

Right then, from behind them, a fire started! It was a small fire that didn't seem to spread. Nobody in the castle had started the fire on purpose, but it wasn't there by accident. Out of the fire, rose the ghostly figure who had stolen their mom. He snarled in a ghastly voice at the old man, and said, "Sacrifice it now, Makamom. Sacrifice it now."

The old man said to the ghostly figure, "Do you really think that your five sons can get it from us?"

"Yes!" said the ghostly figure, and then he disappeared.

"What is this all about?" said Lily to the old man. "Who is Makamom?"

"Makamom is me," said the old man.

"What does he want to steal from you?" asked Lily.

"The Crystal of the Marakon Ways," answered Makamom. "It grants us our powers."

"What about the five sons?" asked Daniel.

"Very well," said Makamom. "I will tell you about the five sons. They are a threat to the Crystal of the Marakon Ways, and they all must be destroyed. The first son of the five sons is Sardrose, the giant spider. The second son is Lavina, the sea serpent. The third son is Extramadan, the lightning man. The fourth son is Archrona, the rock golem. The last son is Death, death himself. Even I fear him. After all, he killed me before."

"What?" asked Lily.

"Yes," said Makamom. "We have ten lives. That's why we're better than cats. And now, I will show you what you came in here to learn: the Marakon Ways. Go, sit down, and I will give you a pleasant show." Makamom said this last part in a soft and sweet voice.

Lily and Daniel took a seat on several pillows on the ground. "The Marakon Ways is a magic martial art used by the people of Wolf Land," Makamom explained. "First, I will show you the fire claw." Lily and Daniel heard the name "fire claw" and thought that he would try to light his hand on fire, but they knew he could not. To both of their surprise, Makamom made a motion and his hand instantly lit up with blue flames! He then jumped high in the air, higher than anyone could imagine. Twenty feet, thirty feet, forty feet, high, high, high he jumped. And then, like falling from the heavens, he plunged down to the castle floor. While he was falling, he slashed at a wooden stick with his fiery hand. It broke with ease.

"We now need to go outside for one of my most amazing stunts," Makamom said to Lily and Daniel, who were still frozen in amazement from the fire claw. They all walked outside. Very slowly, Makamom started to make wind that blew away from the village. Lily and Daniel could see that a tornado was slowly forming. Makamom fell down right before the tornado fully formed.

Makamom wasn't surprised. He said, "I've been working on this technique for 68 years, and I haven't gotten it right one time!"

"Uhhh, Makamom," asked Daniel. "How old are you?"

"Only 487 years old," Makamom answered.

"You're joking," replied Daniel.

"No, I'm not," insisted Makamom. "Now come, there's

something I need to teach you."

Chapter 4

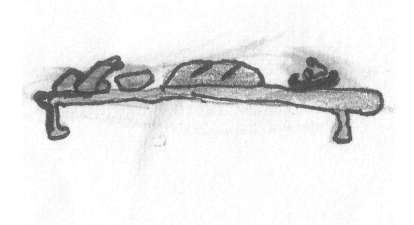

THE ADVENTURE BEGINS

Makamom led Lily and Daniel back into the castle to the room where the twenty chandeliers were still swaying from the roof. There Makamom told them that the reason he wanted to teach them something (as well as what he wanted to teach them, and why) came about because of a prophecy he found deep under the castle while mining for crystals. The prophecy said:

From another land will come two. They are the ones that will end this war and the five sons of Arclos. And they will free our land. Your hope lies on their survival.

From,
Archleny

Lily and Daniel were confused.

"Who is Archleny?" asked Lily.

"Who's Arclos?" asked Daniel.

Makamom said, "Well, Arclos, I don't know exactly who he is. But I know that he is the ghostly figure that we saw earlier, and maybe even the devil himself. He is also the father of the five sons. Arclos once almost stole the Crystal of the Marakon Ways, and he is still trying to get it.

"And now," Makamom continued, "I will tell you about Archleny. He is a good friend of mine. He is out in the War of the Five Sons, trying to defeat Arclos and his sons so we will all be safe. He must have somehow sent the letter containing the prophecy because he knew I would discover it."

Lily and Daniel were amazed at what they had just heard. To break the silence, Daniel asked, "What are you going to teach us?"

"The Marakon Ways," said Makamom. "You must be the ones mentioned in the prophecy who will help us end the war, so we must help you gain the skills you will need. You will only start with simple things, not even exercises, merely control and concentration. Follow me to the Training Room if you wish to learn about the Marakon Ways."

Lily and Daniel were unsure that they could learn the Marakon Ways. But they walked with Makamom into the Training Room. For the rest of the day, Makamom made Lily and Daniel meditate and learn respect. Finally at 5:00 p.m. sharp, Makamom told Lily and Daniel that they were ready to start exercising to become strong as part of their training in the Marakon Ways. However, they would first have to eat dinner and sleep overnight.

"Come with me to the great Feast Hall," said Makamom.

Lily and Daniel followed Makamom, and were stunned when they entered the Feast Hall. The room was large and very bright. There were thousands of wolves and humans seated at tables. In the middle of the room there was a giant fire pit with three cows roasting.

Makamom led Lily and Daniel to their seats. On the table was every type of meat that they could ever imagine: chicken, steak, pork, ground beef, ribs, turkey, bacon, fish, and boar.

"It's so amazing," said Lily.

"Well, then let us feast!" said Makamom.

Lily and Daniel ate and tried every meat in front of them. Oxtail was Daniel's favorite.

After the feast, Makamom led Lily and Daniel to the highest tower in the castle. When he opened the door at the top of the tower, Lily and Daniel gasped. There were thousands and thousands of cells, like jail cells. In each cell, there was a dragon, a cyclops, or a troll. The dragons were huge and ferocious. The cyclops had one eye each and had hammers in their hands. The trolls were ugly and snarled while snot dripped from their noses, with spiky bats in their hands.

Makamom told Lily and Daniel, "These are the jail cells for every evildoers who has ever tried to steal the crystal of the Marakon Ways." But Lily and Daniel noticed one jail cell was empty.

Makamom led them through the narrow pathway to a big room. In the center of the room, on a pedestal, there was the Crystal of the Marakon Ways. The crystal was glowing green.

"This is what they tried to steal. That is why they are in the cells," said Makamom. "If the evildoers destroy it we will lose our powers and then they will defeat us. Now I must show you to your room."

Makamom yelled, "Acseines!" And instantly they were in a big room.

"It's amazing!" said Lily.

"So what?" said Daniel. "Where is the big, flat screen TV?"

"Have you forgotten?" said Lily. "We are in another dimension."

"But seriously, all there is here are pillows, a bed, and a table," said Daniel.

"No," said Lily, "There is also a book right there on the table."

The book Lily referred to was a small, blue book. It didn't look too important, but when Daniel looked closely at it he was stunned by the title: *The History of the Marakon Ways*. When Daniel opened the book to read, the first page he opened to answered his questions about why Arclos was out causing terror instead of in jail for trying to steal the Crystal of the Marakon Ways.

Daniel read:

CHAPTER 1: ARCLOS

Arclos a being of pure evil. He is the only one who almost stole the Crystal of the Marakon Ways, when everybody else who tried could not even lay a foot into the room where the Crystal of the Marakon Ways is kept. He is also the only one to have escaped from Argleon prison.

"So Arclos was once in one of the jail cells that Makamom showed us, and he escaped!" Daniel exclaimed to Lily. Right then Makamom burst through the door.

"Please tell me you didn't read that book on the table," Makamom said.

"Okay we didn't," said Lily sarcastically.

Then Makamom said, "Be serious with me. Did... You... Read... The... Book?"

"Yes," admitted Daniel.

"Oh no, oh no," moaned Makamom. Then he grabbed the book and ran out the door.

"What was that all about?" asked Daniel.

"I don't know," replied Lily.

Lily and Daniel looked around and noticed what time it was on the clock. Well, it wasn't exactly a clock. It was more like a thingy, with twelve handles and one number. And that number didn't really look like a number. It looked more like a squiggly thing of lines. Nonetheless, they could tell that it was around nine o'clock in the evening. So they got into bed and they started to fall asleep.

While they were sleeping, Daniel had a horrible nightmare. He was in a room with only Lily and Makamom. There was a giant eight-legged spider in front of them. The spider was bigger than a house. Behind the spider was something glowing golden. Right then, the spider lunged for them.

With a start, Daniel woke up. It was exactly 7:00 a.m. sharp. Lily was already awake and putting on her clothes. They weren't normal clothes though. They were robes and big thick boots. "How do I look?" said Lily.

"Horrible," said Daniel.

"Hey, that's not very nice," said Lily. "You're going to have to put on these clothes, too. There aren't any different types of clothes in the castle."

Reluctantly, Daniel put on his clothes and walked downstairs with Lily, hoping to have breakfast. When they got downstairs, Makamom met them.

"It's time for our journey!" said Makamom.

Chapter 5

The Chamber of Webs

Lily and Daniel didn't know what to say as Makamom surprised them with news of a journey. Makamom was in a hurry because his top spies had told him that Sardrose, the first son of Arclos, was getting ready to steal the Crystal of the Marakon Ways. Sardrose needed to be stopped.

    Even though they were hungry and not done with their

training, Lily and Daniel were excited to go on the journey. They all walked out of the castle, and went toward the dark, misty forest in the forforest. In the forest, they heard owls hooting and wolves howling. They walked for a long time, to the end of the woods.

At the end of the woods there was a big chamber of spider webs. At the entrance it read, "The Chamber of Webs," which Makamom knew was Sardrose's home.

"Ready?" said Lily.

"You bet!" said Daniel.

They went into the chamber with Makamom. The chamber was covered in spider webs, from top to bottom. From behind them, they heard shrieks that were coming from huge spiders that were as big as desktop computers.

Makamom yelled, "Lily! Daniel! Run!" But Makamom didn't hear any footsteps following this command. When he looked for them, he saw that they had fainted on the ground from hunger. "I should've known," said Makamom. "Humans can't last that long without food or water. Now what am I going to do? How am I going to wake them up? I know, light! I should do fire claw!"

Makamom did the motions for fire claw. As he did them, he noticed his hand wasn't on fire. He thought the cave's moisture and the spider webs must be interfering with the technique. Instead, Makamom tried to use noise to wake Lily and Daniel up. He decided he would pound the ground to make such a loud noise that even people back at the village would hear it. He hit the ground with so much force that Lily and Daniel easily awoke.

"Where are we?" said Daniel woozily.

"I don't know," said Lily equally as woozy.

"Oh no!" said Makamom, seeing they were confused. "We need to get you food and water fast!" He took out of his pouch a bottle of water and some hard stale bread. As Lily and Daniel ate, their memories returned. However, just as that happened, the huge spiders found Makamom.

The huge spiders attacked. Makamom tried to hold them off using the Marakon Ways, but there were too many of them. Lily and Daniel joined the fight. Right before one of the spiders bit Makamom's left leg off, Lily punched the spider and the spider fell down dead. Makamom thanked Lily, and then went back to fight more spiders.

It took Lily time to recover from the punch. Even though she wasn't the one who got punched, her fist hit the stone wall of the cave after hitting the spider, and that badly hurt her knuckles. Lily's hand was bloody and scarred. While Daniel was still fighting the spiders, Makamom snuck by big group of spiders to help Lily. Makamom used a special healing technique that he learned 200 years ago to heal Lily's hand.

Once Lily's hand was completely healed, Makamom joined Daniel to fight the last of the spiders. Lily got up and started fighting some of the huge spiders, too. The battle continued but seemed to be going on a downward slope for Lily, Daniel, and Makamom. With each passing minute they got a little more hurt and cut.

Makamom finally decided that they should try to flee. He said, "Let's flee," and ran down the cave. Lily and Daniel followed Makamom, running as fast as their feet could carry them away from the spiders. The spiders tried to chase the, but eventually the spiders gave up.

"Phew!" said Lily, "I thought we were goners!"

"At least we made it!" said Daniel.

They turned around and saw a big door. Makamom was standing right in front of it. On the door it read, "Sardrose." Lily and Daniel knew that through the door was Sardrose, the eight-legged beast. They did not want to go in. But they also knew that this is what they came here for. So they followed Makamom through the door.

In the chamber it was cold and moist. Lily could not see that well in the dim light. So she grabbed one of the torches from the wall. Makamom lit the torch with his fire claw, which he was able to do even though it was dark and damp because the chamber was so large. But when he lit the torch they wished he hadn't, because now, in the light, they could see a 20 foot tall spider.

Daniel knew that this spider must be Sardrose. He remembered the nightmare he had had just a day ago, and realized it was exactly the same as what was happening right now. But there was no time to think, because right then Sardrose lunged for them. Makamom and Lily managed to dodge the blow, but Daniel was unlucky. He fell down onto the hard stone floor.

"Are you all right?" asked Lily

"I think so," groaned Daniel.

"He's not," said Makamom. "I know about Sardrose's fatal venom. It is unlikely you will survive."

Chapter 6

THE BATTLE, PART 1

Daniel thought he would perish when Makamom told him that Sardrose's venom was fatal. But what he did not know is that there was one way he could survive, and that was if Sardrose was defeated. If any of the five sons were destroyed, they would be imprisoned in the crystal of the Marakon Ways. And then all effects done by that son would go away. And Daniel would survive. Makamom told Lily and Daniel this.

But could Lily and Makamom defeat Sardrose? That was a puzzle Daniel could only hope would be true until the battle was finished. As Daniel watched, Sardrose cornered Makamom and Lily. But Sardrose stopped attacking them right before he finished off Lily and Makamom, even though he easily could have.

And why? Why did he stop? All because he had seen something behind him, something golden, something yellow. Sardrose pounced right back onto the golden object.

Left alone for a moment, Lily and Makamom had time to get up. But right when they got up, Sardrose turned from the golden object and made another fatal lunge. Lily and Makamom both managed to dodge again by jumping out of the way. But to Makamom's surprise, the spider clearly intended for them to dodge this time because right next to them was a sticky web.

There was no hope for any of them. Lily and Makamom were stuck in Sardrose's web and they were going to be defeated. But then Makamom remembered something. In the hugeness of the chamber he was able to do fire claw again! So he lunged out of the webs with his both of his hands on fire, snapping the web in half.

"Now it's your turn, Sardrose!" said Makamom. With his hands still on fire he lunged at the giant spider. But he just bounced off the spider's thick behind like a rubber ball bouncing off a wall. Makamom's fire claw was not strong enough to defeat Sardrose.

Right after Makamom fell, Lily was finally able to get down out of the webs, and she ran to help Makamom. Daniel was still on the floor, poisoned by the fatal venom and struggling to get up. As he started to rise he found himself crawling towards the golden object near where the spider was busy fighting Makamom and Lily.

Then Daniel saw what the golden item was. It was a bracelet up on a pedestal. Small and golden, but not the type of bracelet you could go to a kid's shop and make with beads, nor the type of bracelet where you could go to a jeweler and pay thousands of dollars. No, this bracelet was something else. It was small, probably made out of gold, and something magic about it made Daniel feel like he wanted to wear it very badly. It was a complex bracelet with a gem like a diamond or emerald hanging from the golden chain. Even though he was sick, he slowly crawled over to it and tried to grab it right out of its holding place.

When Daniel touched the bracelet, however, he said, "Owh!" It was as hotter than magma, or at least it felt that way to Daniel. He pulled his arm back in surprise, but then he thought for a second. His hand, which had only touched the bracelet, wasn't burned at all. What if wasn't the bracelet that was hot. What if it was the pedestal that was hot? If he could find a stick he could probably get the bracelet off the pedestal.

Daniel looked at the ground, but there were no sticks and no branches, only rocks. However, Daniel noticed that there were stalactites hanging from the ceiling. He could use one of them instead. But he knew that he was not tall enough to reach the stalactites.

How could he grab one to get the bracelet? He didn't know, but then he remembered where he was and he remembered about Sardrose, the giant spider. He could climb on the back of Sardrose and grab a stalactite.

But how could he get on the back of Sardrose? He was twenty feet tall. Then Daniel remembered being taught once in nature camp that the bigger a spider gets, the stronger its webs gets. He thought he could probably climb Sardrose's webs to get to his back, and from there he could grab a stalactite.

So that's exactly what Daniel did! He ran behind Sardrose and grabbed onto the web shooting out of Sardrose's spinneret. Using the web he swung onto the back of Sardrose, grabbed one of the stalactites off the ceiling, and then swung back down with the web in his free hand. Sardrose was so busy fighting that he did not even notice.

Daniel was exhausted because of the poison venom. But with the stalactite he hoped that he could now get the bracelet. He walked slowly up to the pedestal. He poked the stalactite right under the bracelet. He slowly pulled the stalactite with the bracelet on it away from the pedestal and felt the bracelet. Luckily there was no heat. He put on the bracelet.

Instantly Daniel felt a surge of energy through his body. Dark energy, black magic. Even though he was poisoned, Daniel felt more alive than he ever had before. It was like somehow his whole body was filled with a magic power. This power he felt was black, dark and black. Not like the magic you think of with magic spells and potions. No, this was the type of magic that controls your body. Not the type of magic that you can control, but the type of magic that controls you. Even though he was poisoned, Daniel slowly got up and, with newfound strength, ran at Sardrose.

Chapter 7

The Battle, Part II

While Daniel was finding the bracelet, I should give you some information about what Lily and Makamom were doing. As you may remember, right after they broke free of the web Makamom tried doing fire claw at Sardrose. But he bounced off Sardrose's behind like a rubber ball. Right when Makamom fell to the ground, Lily had just climbed out of the web.

"Are you okay?" Lily asked Makamom.

"I think so," said Makamom. "But how are we going to defeat Sardrose?"

"I don't know" said Lily. "We must find some way to break through his hide."

"We could do this if we could find a relic. A golden relic," said Makamom. "I know of several powerful but dangerous relics. Their owners become very strong and can do many impossible things, but can also be corrupted and make bad decisions. We could find it and use it, but because it is dangerous we must destroy it when we are done."

"How will we manage to locate one?" asked Lily.

"I don't know, but I have heard that some of the five sons guard golden relics," replied Makamom. "Arclos has his sons guard the relics because the relics can be used to defeat them. But I do not know if Sardrose guards a golden relic. He might not. Not all of the five sons do."

"Then how can we be sure that we can get a golden relic and defeat Sardrose before it's too late?" Lily cried.

"We can't," said Makamom. "We will have to take the chance and try to find the golden relic. If there is none, we will most certainly lose this battle."

Makamom and Lily were about to start looking when they noticed a figure running at Sardrose.

"DANIEL!!!" cried Makamom. "What are you doing running at Sardrose? He could KILL you!" When Daniel heard this he just kept running. "That's weird," said Makamom to Lily. "He would normally be smart enough to know that he is about to kill himself."

"How are we going to stop him?" said Lily.

"By making him take off that bracelet!" said Makamom, who had just realized that Daniel was wearing a golden relic. "The bracelet is a golden relic," Makamom explained to Lily. "It is making him reckless. We need to get it off him. But we need to hurry up. He's going to be killed soon if he keeps fighting Sardrose."

"But how are we going to get the bracelet off him?" asked Lily.

"He has a golden relic, so he won't listen to us. I don't know what we should do," said Makamom. "What if we could force him to take off the bracelet?"

"But how will we do that?" asked Lily.

"With mind control!" said Makamom.

"It's worth a try," said Lily.

So Makamom tried to use mind control. But it just bounced right back and he ended up mind controlling himself. This obviously had no effect. But it was still a problem, because Daniel while wearing the golden relic, could not be mind controlled.

Lily and Makamom needed to find another way to get the bracelet off Daniel. "But how? How?" you might ask. And that's exactly what Makamom and Lily were thinking: How? It was a simple question of how. Could they fight him? Could they put him into a trance?

"What? What are we going to do?" said Lily.

"I don't know," said Makamom. "But maybe we can get him to take it off a different way."

"What way?" said Lily.

"I don't know," said Makamom, "but we better think of it fast."

"What about if we were to surprise him and take the bracelet off him by force?" Lily suggested. "If we do that, where should we hide to jump out at him?"

"We don't need to hide," said Makamom, "We can come at him from behind."

"But isn't the bracelet supposed to give the person who wears it the strength of a thousand men?" asked Lily.

"Actually, a thousand and two," said Makamom.

"Blah, blah, blah. Let's just do it," said Lily.

"Ok, but we need to be careful," said Makamom.

So that's just what they did. They snuck behind Daniel. Then Makamom lunged from the left while Lily lunged from the right. Daniel didn't even seem to notice. Makamom took the bracelet with ease. Right when the bracelet fell off Daniels wrist he instantly stopped charging at Sardrose.

"What happened?" asked Daniel with soft spoken concern.

"Uh oh," said Makamom. "Now that the bracelet is off, the poison of Sardrose is working again."

"So hurry up and put on the bracelet so you can destroy Sardrose and save Daniel," said Lily. And that's exactly what Makamom did.

Right as Makamom slid on the bracelet, Sardrose lunged toward the three heroes. They all fell backwards. There was no hope. They were cornered right against the wall. Sardrose lifted his front appendages to attack. But then, like a bird soaring through the sky, Makamom did a fire claw at the stomach of Sardrose. And with the golden relic on Makamom's wrist, fire claw struck with so much force that Sardrose fell back on the ground motionless and then disappeared.

"Woooo!!!! You did it!" said Lily to Makamom. "You defeated Sardrose!"

"There's no time to celebrate," said Makamom. "We better check on Daniel and then leave this wretched place."

"Daniel looks fine to me," said Lily. Now that Sardrose was gone, the venom no longer was poisoning Daniel.

"We had better destroy the bracelet before it corrupts me though," said Makamom. So he lit the bracelet on fire with fire claw and they all walked out of the door.

Right when they took a step outside of the door, the chamber started to collapse. "RUUUNNNN!" yelled Lily. Through the chamber they ran, into the woods, and, at last, into the safety of the village. When they returned, everybody cheered.

Chapter 8

THE CELEBRATION

A party had been planned by the inhabitants of Wolf Land for the return of our three heroes – that is, if they returned. Which they did!

"Let the party start!" said Arclon, the gray man from the zoo, when they arrived at the castle.

"What's going on?" asked Lily to Makamom.

"I think it's a celebration for our defeating of Sardrose!" said Makamom.

"Okay!" said Daniel. "But I really would have thought that everyone would be dead by now."

"Why do you say that?" said Makamom.

"Look behind you and see for yourself," said Daniel.

When Makamom looked he saw the tornado he had created a day ago when showing Lily and Daniel the Marakon Ways was still there. It was a huge and swirling.

"Well, I don't know how to stop the tornado," said Makamom, "but at least there's good news."

"And what is it?" asked Lily.

"I know I finally perfected the technique," replied Makamom.

"And how is that going to help?" said Daniel.

"Well, I could create another tornado to blow the first tornado off course," said Makamom.

"Let's hope that works!" said Lily.

So Makamom slowly started to move his hands back and forth. Then, just as slowly, a tornado started to form. When it hit the other tornado they both started to fight, like two Titans battling in the sky. Slowly they started to move away from the village. The village was saved! "Hurray!" yelled all of the half-wolf, half-human villagers.

Now that the village was saved the party started. There were lots of games and contests. Makamom entered and won every contest.

The morning after the party Lily and Daniel were both excited and sad because they knew that they would have to go home. And that made Lily and Daniel happy and not.

Right when Lily and Daniel awoke, Makamom was waiting by the door to say goodbye. Lily and Daniel walked with Makamom down to the big room of the castle with the thousand rooms and twenty chandeliers. Makamom said goodbye and opened up a portal back to Earth.

"Bye," remarked Lily.

"Bye," remarked Daniel in a sad voice.

They both stepped through the portal. But instead of disappearing, they fell back on to the ground of the castle.

"What happened?" asked Daniel.

Makamom replied, "I think that since you are the chosen ones that you may not leave this realm until all five sons are gone. There are now only four more, and Arclos."

"Well, that means another adventure awaits us," said Lily.

"Let the war be ours to win. Together we will defeat the five sons of Arclos," said Makamom.

ABOUT THE AUTHOR

My name is Griffin Hehmeyer. I am 8 years old and live in Bellevue, Washington. I am the author of this book. I hope that you liked it. When I first started writing the book I was very excited. It took me about seven months to finish, but I had lots of fun. The story was inspired by a number of fantasy and adventure books, such as *The Lord of the Rings*, *Harry Potter*, and *Sleeping Beauty*. I have loved fantasy for my entire life, and I love to hear tales of adventure.

When I first started this book, I had a hard time thinking of ideas. As I got closer to the ending it was easier to think of what to say. I am going to write five more books in this series. I think that you should try to write a book too. It is lots of fun, whether it is a book of less than a page or a book that has more than a hundred pages.

Most of the book was written at The Little School during the 2012 to 2013 school year. My teacher Matt and my teaching assistant Lani both helped me to type the book. My art teacher Sally and my friends in my class helped me draw the illustrations.

My parents' names are Alex Hehmeyer (my dad) and Jaime Teevan (my mom). I also have three younger brothers. Two of them are six-year old identical twins named Cale and Dillon, and one is a four-year old named Brier.

I want to thank everyone who helped me with this book, including: Matt, Lani, Sally, my class, my school, and my parents. This book is dedicated to everybody who has been my friend and my family in my entire life. I hope that my book inspired you.

ILLUSTRATOR CREDITS

14945628R00040

Made in the USA
San Bernardino, CA
09 September 2014